Choosing Your Wand

By Frederick Mason

Choosing your Wand

Frederick Mason

Copyright © 2011 by JCrossBooks.com

ISBN 978-0-9825793-4-3

All portions of this book are the authors own opinion and though they may be similar to other opinions they were conceived by the author. Graphics were obtained through public domain sources.

A special thanks to Wikimedia Commons for providing a source for public domain media.

Portrait of King David with scepter

"If you are looking for darkness, look not here for there is only the light and the tools to heal.

Mankind is not equal, for the knowledgeable stand with stature and the ignorant stand not."

Purpose of a wand

A wand is normally used in addition to, or in relation with a ritual. In most cases the wand is used to focus energy onto or into a subject or substrate. Since different rituals or rites exist, it would not be uncommon for one to possess more than one wand.

A wand may be used outside of rituals as a method of focusing the user's energy or gathering other energy around them for their own benefit. For centuries the use of a wand or even a bauble has been used to heal people as well as to harm others in some dark manor.

A wand can be carried with one to enhance their ability to focus energy in ordinary daily functions. It is said that focus can increase self confidence, memory, reduce stress and enhance other abilities. Focus may even be disseminated onto others.

Focus, being a magic in itself, is a powerful tool. All successful people use focus whether it is of energy or of mind to obtain their goals. Any item can be used to help obtain the focus of one's mind. If it is of nature, then it will draw from the source of power from which it came. Example, a stone may draw from the earth, a shell from the element of water or an acorn may draw from the oak tree.

A wand is one of four most common and important and powerful tools used in rituals. The others tools I am referring to being the cup or challis, the athame and the pentacle.

The Rod of Asclepius

Ptah holding a staff or scepter

4

Charms

A charm is not a wand and its use is different. A charm is used for storage of a spell, of some power or energy. It can be made of anything man made or natural. It can hold good or bad and can release its power at a predetermined time or when it is instructed to. Examples of charms may be a piece of jewelry, a key, basically anything.

The use of a charm is defined by the spell placed within the charm and the spell may last well beyond the life of the spell maker. The power stored within a charm may come from sources completely irrelevant to the spell maker. A living person, animal or plant cannot be a charm, though a spell may be cast upon them.

A wand may be used to place a spell on or to enchant an object to create a charm or fill a charm with energies.

None of the above should be confused with the athame, one of the most powerful tools of ritual and rite. This tool, a double edged knife with a blackened handle, uses many of the same symbolisms that a wand uses.

A tablet from Pella, Cemetery of Agora, now at the Museum of Pella. First half of the 4th century BC. The lead tablet was found rolled in the right hand a dead man. The text is a curse of magical and ritual meaning.

A marked wand

A marked wand refers to personalizing it to increase the energy within it, or that passes through it. It allows the owner of the wand to have a connection beyond the normal. This formal bond will create a connection that is virtually unbreakable. A blood bond lasts until death of either the wand or the wielder.

If someone other than the owner uses the wand, the power may be transferred to the owner inadvertently. In some cases this is good, but when darkness is used, it could be detrimental to the owner. Bonding with your wand can strengthen the power, but at a cost. Protect access to your marked wand.

To mark your wand: a rune or symbol is carved into the wood. Never burn the rune into the wood as this weakens most woods powers. The rune or symbol must reflect the power of the owner. For wands used for specific rites, other runes reflecting or enhancing the rituals may be added. The owner's rune or symbol is a key mark. It would be placed on the wand so as to be covered with the user's finger or thumb while in use.

The owner would place their own blood into this rune. Use just enough blood to color the rune. Water or clear alcohol (such as gin) may be used to thin the blood allowing it to soak into the wood. Never use oil or man made products to thin the blood. Never use an animal's blood or someone else's blood for this. Words or rites may be used at this time as well as chants depending on purpose of the wand.

In many cases the connection can be felt immediately. I've heard this union referred to as a marriage. In some ways this could be an accurate analogy, but I've thought of it as more of a blood oath. A marriage is an oath of sorts so I must agree with the suggestion.

In either case, a sharing of energy, spirit and/or soul may occur. Take marking your wand seriously and consider the outcomes of each use you put it to before moving forward.

Wands for use in rituals

Wands used in specific rituals should be made and decorated for the specific purpose. Runes for the rite would be carved into the wand to be visible (not covered by the hand) during the rite. The runes chosen would have symbolisms reflecting the goal. For example, a rite of protection may have the Celtic Isa rune or Algiz rune placed in the mid area of the shaft. It may have an Elder handle with a cedar shaft.

Runes used for rites may be dyed using herbs or other trees and plants of which their power would enhance the strength and focus of the wand. The number of runes or symbols decorating the wand is limited only by the knowledge of the owner or end user of the wand. The types of runes or symbols may very as well. Runes and symbols may be Greek, Celtic, and other languages including Native American. The very powerful dream catcher for instance has long been a protection.

Other decorations may be placed on the wand such as metal working. The art of alchemy has commonly been mingled with the power of the four elements and may, in some cases, enhance the powers of a wand. Insets in a true useable wand must never be glued or cemented in place. Friction locking such as keyhole locks or brads may be used. The most effective uses are not intrusive to the wood. For example, a silver snake may be wrapped around the wand so that its power works beside or parallel to the wand and not through it. The spiral of the snake or a vine has long symbolized consciousness and growth in different cultures.

The medical industry today used a snake around the rod of Aesculapius (called the Caduceus). Another medical association uses a rod with two snakes along with the wings of Mercury. Actually snakes and dragons have very powerful symbolisms in a great deal of cultures.

Many cultures use gems and other stones to adorn some of the larger staffs and scepters. I've included what I've found to be some common personalities of gems and metals in the indexes.

The wood

For centuries trees have symbolized different strengths of mankind. These symbols have been well documented in Europe. Less documentation has been kept in the United States. Many trees in Europe exist in other places, though they may be of a different variety, but they are of the same or similar strength in conductance. A list of trees and their symbolisms are in the indexes.

Typically wands have been made with a single type of wood. This has been a very effective method of building wands and a powerful tool. Use of multiple woods has been used in wands by the most powerful masters. Wands may be carved in levels and fitted together as dowels or mortis and tenon. This allows the combination of different types of wood. When woods are laminated together with an adhesive, it is important to use an adhesive that is natural and completely without man made materials or processed petroleum products.

Collecting wood for building a wand should be a carefully thought out method. Some woods are strengthened by the moon and should be collected in the light of the full moon. The willow tree must receive a gift before harvesting

11

wood for a wand as it is bad luck to steal from this very powerful feminine figure. Refer to the appendix for a list of harvesting methods.

Trees blown over or loss of limbs due to wind have a strong connection to the element of wind. Trees or branches washed away in flood waters have a strong connection to the element of water. The same can be said about a landslide and the element of earth. Lightening would be connected with the element of fire. These woods may not need a core to have the strength of an element.

Choosing a wood for your wand can be done in various ways. The Celts established a calendar of the trees. It is much like the zodiac with each type of tree spanning several days. This calendar is included in the indexes.

A time honored method is to go out into the woods and connect with the trees yourself. Lean against a tree for a while and see what energy you feel. When you feel the right energy, identify the type tree and you have made the choice. Note that as people are all different, it is impossible to explain how you will feel. If you are in tune with your mind and body, you will know the "magic", or feeling. Some may feel total harmony; others may feel a stir of restlessness.

In some cases the tree has chosen the person. I once witnessed a branch of a tree fall striking the right arm of a woman. I thought, could this be a case where the tree chose this person?

The most common method is that of tradition. Learning the symbolisms, the rites and rituals, that has been passed through the centuries giving the wand very stable strengths.

Depending on one's personal beliefs, it is not uncommon to use any wood and not even know what it is. As long as what is used is in balance with the user, then the energy can flow freely. Actually, balance is something that we all must strive for in any relationship.

The core

The core of a wand is a subject debated in recent years. A master's wand using multiple woods may have a core imbedded within it. Cores are typically of the four elements; earth, water, fire or wind. The material used as a core may be pulverized, mixed with sap or honey and sealed into a void within the wand. It may be mounted on the end of a staff as an adornment. There are no rules for this. Core does not mean it is within; in this case it is as a center for power or the transference or control of power.

The owner of the wand may chant over a lake or stream and pick a leaf carried to them on the water, thus the element of water is used as the core by placing the leaf within the wand. The same may apply to a feather blown in on a breeze. A stone from a volcano may represent the elements of fire and of earth.

Core material may be used to dye runes on the wand. As long as the core material is of one of the four elements, then the power and energy of that (or those) element(s) will be combined into the wands. Keep in mind that the elements are much stronger than the power of the wood itself since the elements are the basic building blocks. The elements have their power stored within; the wood directs and conducts or focuses these powers (and others) toward a cause or common goal.

In many sects, the use of salt is a direct connection to the earth. Salt water, such as sea water, is a direct connection to the element of water. In many areas, the wand itself symbolizes the element of wind.

The use of parts of a unicorn or a phoenix makes for great fiction, but the use of any animal or insect part for a core element leads in darker directions. Bringing harm or death to a creature for personal use is not viewed as a positive thing. Objects given freely by a creature, on the other hand, are a positive thing. A feather left by a bird or the remnants of an egg from hatched turtles, even a discarded spider web can be considered as positive signs and make a great core.

More than one core is possible. How you bring it all together must be carefully thought out. Some elements complement others as some fight others. Water will extinguish fire, for example. Water and earth create a flourishing environment for growth. How you mix and match the strengths of your wand must also be very personal. Never forget that the wand is an extension of yourself and your strengths, feelings and dreams.

With that information, understand that a wand will function well without a core and in fact, most wands have no core. The core adds its own power into the mix and its power must then be calculated into the outcome. In some cases a core may cause damage to an otherwise simple ritual. Only a fool dabbles in powers that they do not understand. The wood of the wand may be considered a conduit, but a core of elemental material adds its power assisting the wood to perform its job.

The finish

I have been asked many times about the finish of a wand. Can I use stain? How about a coat of polyurethane? Is lacquer an acceptable finish? I cannot stress this enough, nature has its own power and it must not be weakened by unnatural materials. Stains can be manufactured by your own hands for free and you know what is in it. Beauty is only skin deep but the contamination may run throughout.

If any oil must be used make sure it comes from a plant. Linseed oil comes from flax seed and is natural. Do not use boiled linseed oil as petroleum products are added into the mix. Be cautious of Tung oil as most of it these days is not actually from the Tung tree.

Wax is one answer. Bees wax is the original sealer. You'll find that it wears off and it will need to be maintained. It can be obtained where bees are kept or where leather craft supplies are sold. Some hobby stores sell bees wax, but I'm not sure of the purity of it. With a clean dry cloth or wool, rub the wax in firmly until no residual amount is left. It will shine and have a pleasing odor as well.

Any natural material may be used to enhance the look, feel or even the smell of your wand. I know personally many wands have no finish at all.

Small bricks of beeswax purchased from an apiary. This is about a pound shown on a common dinner plate.

How the magic works

For as long as the world has been in existence, there has been a power that makes things change and grow. The heat of the sun is energy in itself. Life on this planet uses this energy to grow and change. Many people see it as God or gods. Some do not see anything at all.

In the Middle Ages mankind saw the use of knowledge as magic. When herbs were used to heal someone, it was magic. Anything that was creative, scary, or not understood became magic. As the Church grew powerful, magic became viewed as evil. Some believe the Church feared the knowledge possessed by these artisans and did what they could to stop them.

During all this time the magic of focused energy has been used by people. Some people use this magic without even knowing it. Example, a businessman leaves on Friday to sit out in the woodland to release all his stress and returns on Monday energized and ready for work. Whether he realizes it or not, the power of the trees did their job, like magic.

Magic is all about the mind as well. When dealing with people, the power of suggestion is magic itself. The mind is a powerful organ and is capable of many things. Many spells must be known by the recipient for them to properly work. This is because the power of suggestion is part of the magic. Basically, the focus of the spell maker and the recipient are both used to achieve a goal.

In healing a person, the mind plays the largest part. Most of the healing powers come from within the beneficiary. An herb will go so far to heal a person, but the belief that one is being healed will carry them through. The use of a wand makes the power more tangible for some.

Positive energy can be passed on through rites, rituals and meditation. It can also be propagated in other means. Some people may not be convinced that a ritual may be needed, and that's okay. A simple conversation or just positive reinforcement can do a lot.

If a medical doctor uses a placebo, it is as if he uses a wand of sorts, and through the power of the mind, transferred via the placebo, the energy heals. The positive support may make the patient hold on long enough to get them where they need to be.

As stated before, the wand is an extension of one's self. As you bond with your wand, connections will be made to parts of yourself that may not even be realized. As you decorate your wand with runes or symbols, you may find the powers of these feeding back to you from the wand. Power and energy will flow both directions (in and out).

You may feel emotions that you would normally not feel. When this occurs, use your head and don't allow these feelings or emotions to rule over you. Though the wand is an extension of you, you must not allow it to have power over you, just as you would not allow your hand to do things against your will. One must learn to work with the wand as if it were another limb or an organ within.

Carrying your wand with you may give you strengths that exceed common people's abilities. It may give you better focus, self confidence or simply allow the wielder to better understand something. It will be a presence to the wielder as if a brother or sister were with them. It may allow sight beyond what is seen. A wand could give you physical strength or a better memory. Magic is endless.

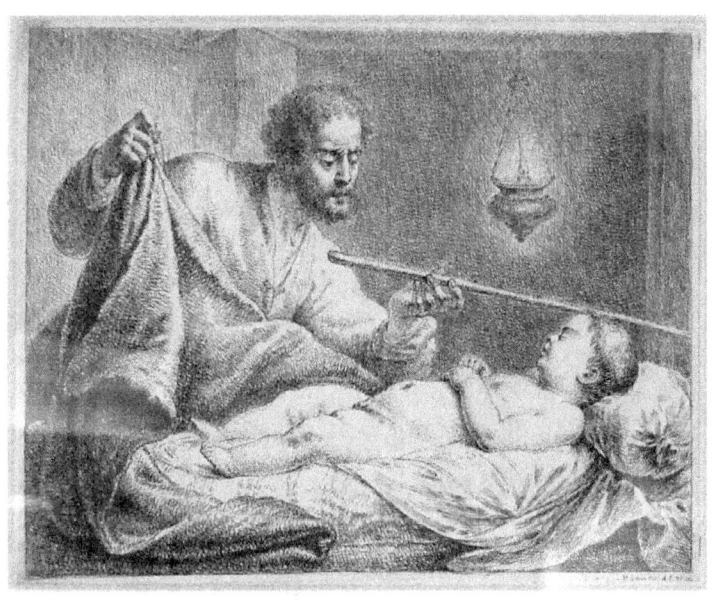

Gehazi attempts to awaken a child with the staff of
Elisha. Engraving by Bernhard Rode, 1700s

Length of a wand

This subject has been the subject of many heated debates recently. In reality wands have been many sizes and shapes. Water witchers use forked sticks up to three and four feet in length. Free masons used walking sticks as tall as eight feet in height as a wand among other uses. In some rituals wands have been as small as a person's finger. For the Baresman's ritual the bundle of rods used must not be taller than a man's knee.

Several things should be considered when deciding a length for ones wand. Symbolism has many times been the key in this area. Many people today think that a 13-inch wand is a symbolic length. The important thing is that the end use or user must decide the size and shape and in fact the entire design of the wand and be comfortable with it.

A wand can even be a bauble. A bauble defined in this case as a small piece of jewelry, ornament, a stone or almost anything small enough to hold in the palm of one's hand. It must be natural and not manmade such as plastic and such. A bauble used in lieu of a wand is not to be confused with a charm. A wand is what it is and the shape is up to the user.

The word "wand" has been traced back to mean a shaft or stick. As time goes on, the same words were used to mean scepter or rod. In any case it all could be defined to mean power. A scepter means power. A rod, even for a shepherd is power over his flock, even ancient Egyptians priests and their kings had rods of power and office. They also had amulets that may well have been used as wands since amulets were used to symbolize power.

When you choose your wand from among many, hold it in your hand and focus on the energy within yourself and within the wand. A bond must be felt between the two as if meeting someone for the first time. First impressions are everything because the communication is of pure energy. Handle it with both hands and hold it against you. Point the wand sending your energy through it to see if you communicate well.

Usually the perfect wand will be felt immediately. Other wands in one's collection may need more time as they have specific uses and may work the best during certain rites or rituals. Be comfortable with a new wand before you keep it as your own.

If you are constructing a wand, take the raw materials and feel their power as well. All parts must be natural and you can sing to them or chant over them as you bring it all together. From the time when the materials are collected to the time of completion it is almost like giving birth. The events are memorable and each wand you make is unique and special. As children, they each have their own personality and they are each a part of you.

Enjoy the pleasures of your work and the reality of your dreams and the warmth of nature.

Reproduction of the Magic Circle by John William
Waterhouse painted in 1886.

Wands and technology

Setting aside that magic and science have always been closely linked, this subject must be addressed. Some master wand makers today use tools that are very technologically advanced. Therefore the question arises as to how this is a natural method of creating something that uses or conducts the natural magic?

Evidence has been found that ancient Egyptians as early as 2700 years before Christ had fabricated wood turning lathes. They turned scepters, rods and other items with a proficiency that must be respected even today. I see no difference in using today's tools to accomplish the same thing. A set of carving tools accomplish the same thing a wood lathe does, only taking different skills to do so. The carving tools of today are manufactured using technology that wasn't dreamed of a century ago.

The only question left is the use of electricity as an energy that is directly applied to a wand. A lathe physically spins the wood for the craftsman to shape. The question therefore is valid. This question can only be answered by the end user as that is who it affects. If you have this question, then your belief should be respected and you should not use this method of wand making.

I am a firm believer that some people can feel energies that others cannot. This does not make them stronger or weaker, but it does make them different. These differences are what make us strong.

Index of wood

Alder – Alder is said to be strong with a core of fire, however it works well with all four of the elements. It has a strong masculine personality.

No special harvesting criteria found.

Celtic – Wholeness.

Apple – This tree symbolizes strong family values and has been used primarily for fertility. Its personality is feminine.

No special harvesting criteria found.

Celtic – Love, peace & fertility

Christian – Tree of good and evil

Ash – It has been said that Ash is a father to the trees. Its strongest core is of the element of water. As a father, it is masculine. It draws from the moon and works best during the strong phases of the moon.

If harvesting from a live tree, the tree must see the reflection of the moon in water. If a branch is collected from the water, it must see the moon before it is made into a wand.

Celtic – Protection, health

Birch – A relative of the Oak, Birch shows its strength in exploring new places. It enjoys starting anew. It has strong ties to the element of fire.

The sun must be strong on the day this wood is acquired. A cloudless day when the sun is at its apex.

Celtic – Purifying, protect youth

Christian – Fertility (May pole is Birch)

Blackthorn - Blackthorn has the power to alter fate and cause people to perform actions they have no power over.

Collect on the winter solstice without spilling any of your own blood. If a thorn pricks you, you must leave the tree intact.

Celtic – Strife and war

Christian – Tree of witches and evil

Cedar – Cedar is known as a tree of life. He is very adept of drawing energy from the earth. This tree grounds and stabilizes other powers. This tree has a masculine personality as well.

The wood for a wand must be collected from a live cedar tree. Take only one branch that touches the earth.

Christian – Cleansing (Hebrew – to be firm)

Elder – Elder, also known as the crucifixion tree, gives its user confidence, eloquence and a calmness that few others can. Elder wands help drive away evil spirits and can help one see the "little people". The Elder tree is feminine and its wood is heartless.

No special harvesting criteria found.

Celtic – Rebirth and regeneration

Christian – Compassion and zealousness

Elm – Elm is the tree of the faeries. No marks shall be burned into it or a curse will be upon you. Elm adds insight and foundation. Elm resists the element of water. He is masculine.

Harvesting should take place where several Elms stand.

Christian – Dignity and faithfulness

Hawthorn – This tree has a confused symbolism. It promotes potency in men yet enforces chastity in women. It is strong in self preservation and can be used for cleansing. It is a masculine tree.

No special harvesting criteria found.

Celtic – Prosperity, fertility, harmony

Holly – The Holly tree by its very name means holy and consecrated. It also stands for beauty and for wealth. This means it can go different directions, depending on how it is used. The Holly tree is masculine.

Collect only on the winter solstice.

Celtic – Spirituality, protection

Christian – Christ crown of thorns

Juniper – He is the creator of visions and promotes lust of the holder. The burning of branches were said to protect against witches and their spells. This is a masculine tree as well.

Collect only in the winter season.

Celtic – Protection from evil

Christian – Advent

Native American – Western region (Navajo)

Oak – The Oak is of the kings and stands for strength. It holds and controls fire and lightening. It is very strong in battle. It is of course masculine.

When cutting from the tree, do this on the summer solstice. When collecting from the elements, anytime is fine. (I.e. limbs blown down from wind)

Celtic - Leadership

Peach – The Peach is a symbol of marriage and stands for fruitfulness and abundance. It is gentle kind and soothing to the soul. She is feminine.

Collect on the full moon nearest the beginning of spring.

Pine – Pine is the symbol of immortality and of life. It is very basic and soothing. It too is masculine.

No special harvesting criteria found.

Celtic - creativity, life, longevity & immortality

Native American – Peace (white pine)

Rowan – An empowering personality.

Celtic – Empowerment, health

Willow – The moon owns her and is the master of enchantment. The Willow is known for its ability to make wishes come true. It is truly feminine.

Collect the willow only on the full moon. She must grant you permission and a gift must be left to repay what has been received

Celtic – Health, protection, fertility

Christian – The gospel

Native American – Wisdom

Yew - The Yew is known as the tree of death. It is the sister of the Silver Fir, who controls rebirth. The binding of these two trees has the power of the light and the dark. Yew must never be used alone as death surrounds it. It is used to enhance other powers, especially visions, psychic abilities and divination. This tree is feminine.

It must only be collected on the spring solstice.

Celtic – Power, Honor, Mystery, Illusion, Worship, Strength, Sanctity

Index of American trees

Beech – This selfish personality has been jealous of the virtues of the Oak. It symbolizes the strength in communication and the skill in ones labors. The Beech tree overpowers the wind with strong ties to the element of earth. He is masculine.

Collect not from a young tree. The time is when the hair is no longer on the bottom of its leaves.

Magnolia – An American tree with symbolism from a Christian background – Gentile, family and beauty. This is a feminine personality.

No special harvesting criteria found.

Maple – This masculine presence has a love affair with the element of water. He likes to stay where he is and dominates his area. The Boxelder is a close kin with like properties.

No special harvesting criteria found.

Redwood – These massive trees though not a hardwood grow to gargantuan sizes. The Native Americans likened them to a bear to indicate great size and strength but gentle in nature.

No special harvesting criteria found.

Silver Fir – This is the tree of birth and of rebirth. This tree gives strength to the very young and when mixed with other trees, gives light and youthfulness. This tree has a feminine personality.

She must only be collected during the birth of a child and the needles must be burned at the home of the new born.

Index of Celtic tree calendar

Index of Celtic runes

A – Ansuz   **ᚠ**   Eloquence

B – Berkano   **ᛒ**   Beginnings

C, K – Kanaz   **ᚲ**   Inspiration

D – Dagaz   **ᛞ**   Emergence

E – Ehwaz   **ᛗ**   Motion

F – Fehu   **ᚥ**   Wealth

G – Gebo   **ᚷ**   Exchange

H – Hagalaz   **ᚺ**   Loss

I – Isa   **ᛁ**   Preservation

J – Jera   **ᛃ**   Years

C, K – Kanaz   **ᚲ**   Inspiration

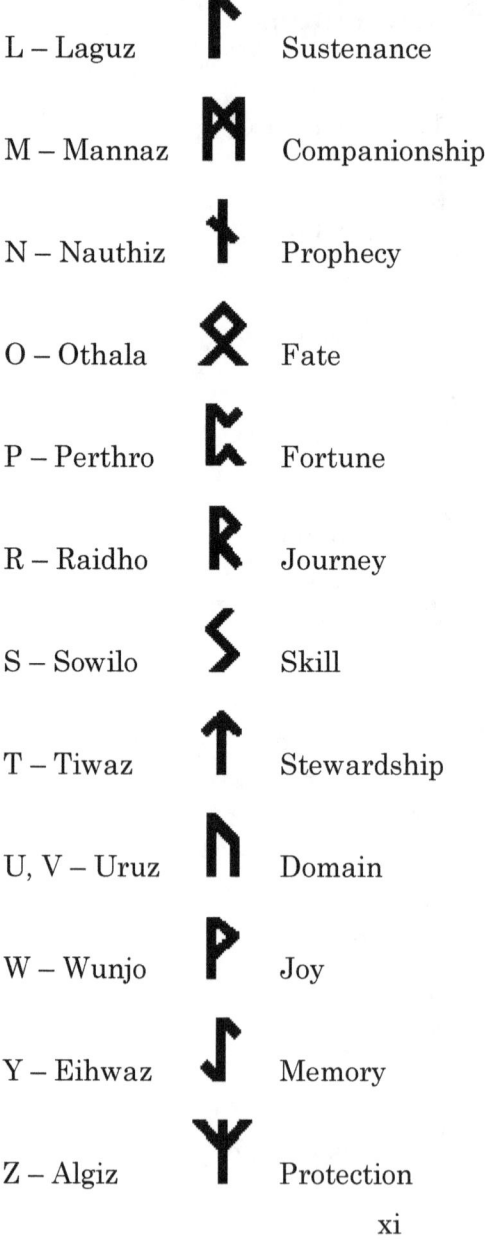

L – Laguz		Sustenance
M – Mannaz		Companionship
N – Nauthiz		Prophecy
O – Othala		Fate
P – Perthro		Fortune
R – Raidho		Journey
S – Sowilo		Skill
T – Tiwaz		Stewardship
U, V – Uruz		Domain
W – Wunjo		Joy
Y – Eihwaz		Memory
Z – Algiz		Protection

TH – Thurisaz ᚦ Thorn

NG – Ingwaz ◆ Arrival

Index of Greek alphabet

α – alpha – a – Apollo says you will do everything successfully

β – beta – b – With the help of Fate, you will have an assistant, Apollo

γ – gamma – g – The Earth will give you the ripe fruit of your labors

δ – delta – d – In customs, inopportune strength is weak

ε – epsilon – e – You desire to see the offspring of righteous marriages

ζ – zeta – z – Flee the very great storm, lest you be disabled in some way

η – eta – e – The Sun, who watches everything, watches you θ – theta – th – You have the helping Gods of this path

ι – iota – I – There is sweat and it excels more than everything

κ – kappa – k – To fight with the waves is difficult; endure, friend

λ – lamda – l – The one passing on the left bodes well for everything

μ - mu – m – It is necessary to labor, but the change will be admirable

ν - nu – n – The strife-bearing gift fulfils the oracle

ξ - xi – x – There is no fruit to take from a withered shoot

o – omicrom – o – There are no crops to be reaped that were not sown

π – pi – p – Completing many contests, you will seize the crown

ρ – rho – r, rh – You will go on more easily if you wait a short time

σ – sigma – s – Phoibos speaks plainly, "Stay, friend"

τ – tau – t – You will have a parting from the companions now around you

υ – upsilon – u – The affair holds a noble undertaking

φ – phi – ph – Having done something carelessly, you will thereafter blame the Gods

Χ – chi – kh – Succeeding, friend, you will fulfill a golden oracle

Ψ – psi – ps – You have this righteous judgment from the Gods

ω – omega – M – You will have a difficult harvest season, not a useful one

*Text is from the Olympian Oracle.

Index of Native American symbols

The Clouds, Rain & Lightning. Representing themselves. They are important symbols for change, renewal & fertility. Related to snow which is a higher blessing than rain.

The Morning Star. The brightest star on the dawn's horizon. Considered an important spirit and honored as a kachina with most Pueblo Indians. Plains and the Great Basin Indians honored it as a sign of courage and purity of spirit. The Ghost Dance Religion associated it as a symbol of the coming renewal of tradition and resurrection of past heroes. Other spirits are sometimes represented as stars.

The Sun. Life giver. Warmth, growth, and all that is good & well. The rays signify the 4 directions in this design.

The Zia. Named for Zia Pueblo, who first used it, it is another symbol of the sun, and also of the 4 directions and the repetition of life on earth. Also may be associated with the place of emergence.

The Frog. Water animal, implies renewal, fertility & springtime.

The **Bear**. Protector. Physical strength & leadership. Frequently mentioned as "first helper" in creation & emergence stories.

The **Deer**. Hunting prey animal, sacrificial and sometimes mentioned as "first helper" in a few emergence stories, also family protection and speed.

The **Horned Lizard**. Significant in some Navajo stories implying perseverance and keeping past secrets. An old saying is "they'll steal your eyes if you look at them too much!"

The **Tadpole**. Immature frogs implying fertility and renewal. They can change and are considered very powerful because of this.

The Turtle. A water animal. Strength, feminine "power fetish" animal, fertility, long life & perseverance. Considered by many to be able to defy death, also an annoyance to the Coyote

The Coyote. This trickster is a powerful hunting prey god and fetish. Very keen to find things, often considered as an omen that something not pleasant could happen.

The Dragonfly. Associated with water & springtime. Also considered a messenger as well.

Dragonfly Forms. Shown is an abstraction of the dragonfly, which can be used as a talisman, especially with the Southern Pueblo Indians. At Isleta it became a double armed cross. This was worn as a symbol of both Catholic conversion and respect for older traditions.

The Cricket. A singer. Connected with fertility, water and springtime.

The Badger & Bear Paws. Badger is shown here. Known as a way of summoning the power of the animal spirit & as a sign of the presence of the spirit. Badgers are honored as healing animals and tenacious hunters. Their tracks can signify strength & well being. Tracks are also considered symbols of leadership & authority.

The Wolf Track. And other predator's tracks signify a direction rather than the spirits presence. These are also symbols of authority and leadership. Used as a clan symbol.

The Deer Track. Symbols of prosperity, well being, safety and the abundance of prey. Directional indicator and as a clan symbol.

Kokopelli, the seed bringer and water-sprinkler (a reference to his male anatomy), is a common fertility symbol throughout the Southwest. He is a personage who is honored as a kachina by most Pueblo cultures. He is associated with fertility, the male principal and physiology, and the concept of the significance of protecting seeds. Usually depicted as old, bent under his heavy load, he visits various communities, impregnating the young women drawn to the tones of his flute playing.

Index of Gems

Abalone – Versatile personality

Agate – Strong and courageous, also a powerful healer

Alexandrite – Self confident

Amber – Promotes balance in life

Amethyst – Self control

Ametrine – Searches for inner truth

Amazonite – Balances the battles between the mind and heart

Apatite – Makes clear the balance between healing and humanity

Aquamarine – Inner spiritual growth

Aventurine – Washes away impurities of the mind and soul

Azurite – Insight

Bloodstone – Balances energy of the heart

Calcite – See the stars

Celestine – Positive personality

Citrine – Tolerant

Coral – Adaptable

Diamond – Faithful and dedicated

Dioptase – Maintains focus by use of wisdom

Emerald – Insight into dreams and faces fears

Fluorite – Calm in the face despair

Garnet – Commitment to self and others

Gold – Balance in all things and learns from experience

Gypsum – Loves to learn

Hematite – Attains focus through organization

Jade – Unconditional love

Jasper – Strong protector and grounds energy through humanity

Malachite – Acceptance in what is unchangeable

Moonstone – Harmony, kindness and concern

Obsidian – Protector of the weak and shield from negative energy

Onyx – Fortuity and self-control

Opal – Decisive and spontaneous

Pearl – Integrity and balanced

Peridot – Clear minded

Platinum – Intuitive and confident

Pyrite – Seer of truth

Quartz

Clear – Amplifies the conductance of all energies

> Phantom Quartz – Aware of the original truth
> Rose Quartz – Balanced in emotion
> Rutilated Quartz – Healer of the body from injury
> Smoky – Survival instinct

Rhodonite – Strong chi

Ruby – Strength of heart

Sapphire – Beauty and intuition

Silver – Relaxation (of the moon)

Sodalite – Endurance and peaceful

Sugilite – Euphoria

Tanzanite – Insight into unseen

Tiger Eye - Commitment

Topaz – Collector of cosmic energy

Tourmaline

> Clear or White – Enhancement of other energy
> Blue – Compassion
> Pink – Love
> Green – Sumptuousness
> Yellow – Willing to change
> Orange – Creativity
> Black – Reality

Turquoise – Attune to all spirituality

Unakite – Logical

Vanadinite – Naturalist

Zircon – Attuned to the laws of nature